GOLDILOCKS AND THE THREE BEARS

REIMAGINED!

REIMAGINED BY

Jerry Popowich
& Doug Sinclair

ILLUSTRATED BY

Maria Kiriakova

INSTRUCTIONS

1

DOWNLOAD THE FREE MOBILE APP!

Scan the QR code or visit www.incredebooks.com/apps. Look for the Goldilocks and the Three Bears - Reimagined app and download the app on your iOS or Android device.

2

READ, THEN LOOK FOR SPECIAL PAGES!

Read the book and look for this symbol on special pages. There are four pages that contain special 3D games!

3

WATCH THE PAGES COME TO LIFE IN 3D!

Launch the app and hold your smart phone or tablet facing the book page that contains the symbol. Make sure the entire page is visible. Now watch the page come to life in 3D!

FIND OUT MORE INFORMATION AT WWW.INCREDEBOOKS.COM

Once there were three bears:
Papa Bear, Mama Bear, and little Baby Bear.
Those weren't their real names, but their real names
are hard to say if you're not a bear.

One day, the bears left their house
in the woods to go visit Uncle Bear,
who lived at the city zoo.

Baby Bear was very excited, because he had never been away from their house before.
He wanted to see what something that was not their house looked like.

You might be surprised to learn that bears are allowed to take the bus.

They are not, however,
very good at reading bus schedules.
So they took entirely the wrong bus.

When they got off, they found themselves
in a strange part of the city with many tall buildings
and very few zoos. After wandering for a while,
they became hopelessly lost.

They decided to ask for help at the next place they could find... which turned out to be apartment #1705 on the 17th floor of a very tall apartment building. That didn't matter, because they were really lost.

They knocked, but nobody was home. The door
was not locked, and inside it was warm and
tastefully decorated. So, they decided they
would stay and wait for whoever lived there to
come home and give them directions.
Of course, anybody would do that upon arriving
home to find live bears in their apartment.

Throughout the apartment were
pictures of a girl with beautiful,
long golden hair.

12

Baby Bear liked her, and called her Goldilocks.

That was not her real name, but it is hard say a person's real name when you're a bear. It's even harder when you don't know their real name.

Soon, they grew hungry. Papa Bear looked in
the kitchen and found a big pot of porridge,
right on the stove.

At least, he thought it was porridge, even though
it was red and had vegetables and pasta in it.
Papa Bear loved porridge, and he thought that
was all anybody ever cooked in a pot.

Papa Bear tasted it.
"This porridge does not have enough
creamy oatmeal," he said.
Mama Bear tasted it. "This porridge has
too much oregano and pepper," she said.

Finally, Baby Bear tasted it. "This porridge is just right, but it's not porridge," he said, "it's minestrone soup," and he ate it all up, because he was tired of porridge all the time.

The bears continued to wait, but they soon got tired of standing around. So, they decided to have a seat in the big puffy chair they found in the living room.

All the chairs at the bears' house in the forest were made out of creaky wood and spiky pinecones by Papa Bear. So, this big soft chair seemed very strange to them.

Papa Bear sat down.
"This chair has too much soft cushioning," he said.
Mama Bear sat down.
"This chair leans back too far," she said.

Baby Bear sat down, "This chair vibrates!"
he said as he turned it on. "It's juuuuuu...
...uuuu...
...uuuu...
...uuuust right!" It was nice to sit without a
spiky pinecone jabbing him in the behind,
for a change.

It was now late afternoon and the bears were getting very sleepy. Back home, they slept on hard wooden beds that squeaked and gave them slivers. Here, all they could find was a big, plush bed that couldn't possibly give you a sliver—even if it tried!

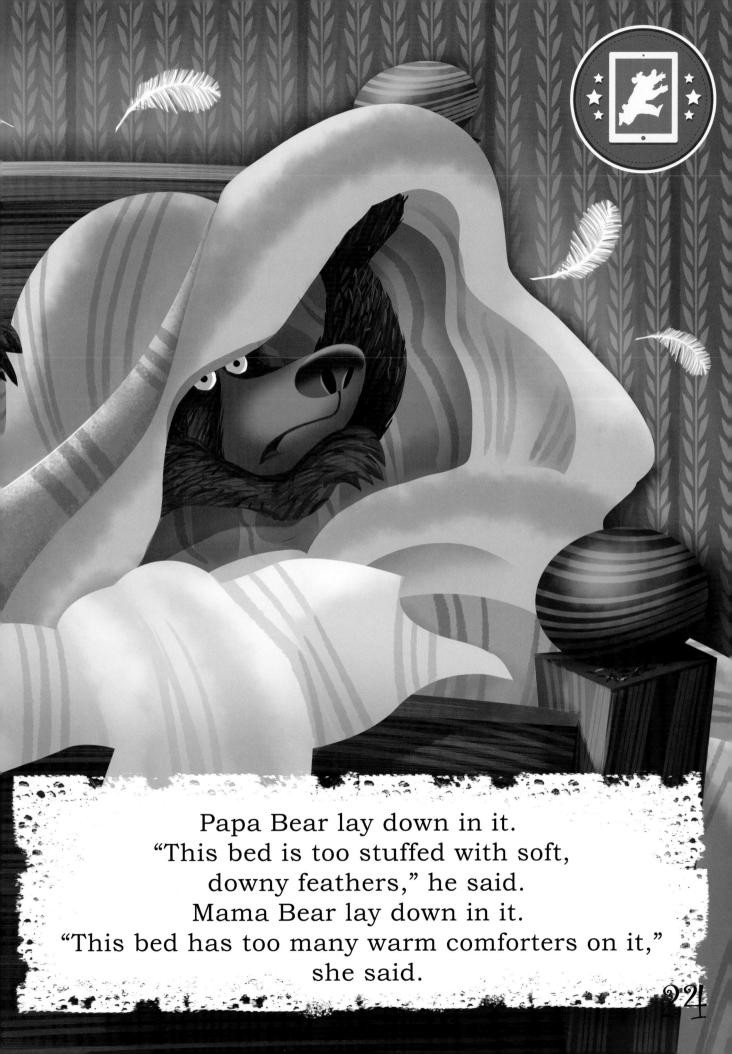

Papa Bear lay down in it.
"This bed is too stuffed with soft,
downy feathers," he said.
Mama Bear lay down in it.
"This bed has too many warm comforters on it,"
she said.

Baby Bear was fast asleep in the vibrating chair...so he didn't try the bed at all.

Just then, Goldilocks got home after a long day at school. Can you imagine her great surprise when she found all her soup gone and her bed messed up?

The bears in her apartment were a little surprising too...

"Please," said Papa Bear, "we are lost,
and just want to visit
Uncle Bear at the zoo. Can you help us?"

Lucky for them, Goldilocks was a very nice girl.
And although she didn't speak bear,
somehow she could tell that they needed her help.

So she took them all to the zoo where they all had
a lovely picnic with Uncle Bear.
People aren't normally allowed in the cage
with big hungry bears,
but Goldilocks' picnic looked so yummy,
nobody worried that the bears would eat her instead.

It was now time for the three bears to return home. Goldilocks took them to the bus station and made sure they got on the right bus.

Only, Baby Bear didn't want to leave.
He liked Goldilocks and her luxury
apartment on the 17th floor. And so,
she promised him that he could come
and visit her whenever he wished.

"Thank you," said all the bears to Goldilocks.
Because whether you're a bear or a person,
it's never hard to say "thank you".

Goldilocks sent the bears on their way home and gave them some gifts to take too...And they all lived happily ever after.

The End